SAVED BY THE SHELL!

Based on the screenplays "Day One, Part One" and "Day One, Part Two,"
by Joshua Sternin and Jeffrey Ventimilia

Illustrated by Patrick Spaziante

Random House 🏠 New York

© 2012 Viacom International Inc. and Viacom Overseas Holdings C.V. All rights reserved.
Published in the United States by Random House Children's Books, a division of Random House, Inc.,
1745 Broadway, New York, NY 10019, and in Canada by Random House of Canada Limited, Toronto.
Random House and the colophon are registered trademarks of Random House, Inc. Nickelodeon,
Teenage Mutant Ninja Turtles, and all related titles logos, and characters are trademarks
of Viacom International Inc. and Viacom Overseas Holdings C.V.
Based on characters created by Peter Laird and Kevin Eastman.
ISBN: 978-0-307-98071-7
randomhouse.com/kids
Printed in the United States of America
10 9 8 7 6 5 4 3 2 1

For fifteen years, four turtle brothers lived beneath the streets of New York City. In a secret lair in the sewers, Splinter, their martial arts teacher, trained them to be ninjas.

When Splinter thought Leonardo, Raphael, Michelangelo, and Donatello were ready, he allowed them to go aboveground for the first time.

New York City was dark and dirty—and the Turtles loved it!

The city was filled with incredible surprises. The best one was . . . pizza!

"I never thought I'd taste anything better than worms and algae," said Raphael. "This is amazing!"

"It's great up here," said Michelangelo.

As the Turtles headed back to the sewer, they saw a girl walking with her dad. Her name was April.

"She's the most beautiful girl I've ever seen," Donatello said.

"She's the *only* girl you've ever seen," Leonardo replied.

Suddenly a van screeched to a stop. Strangers jumped out and grabbed April and her dad. The Turtles rushed to help, but they kept bumping into each other. Leonardo hit Raphael. Michelangelo tripped over Donatello. While the Turtles were tangled up, the strangers escaped with April and her dad.

One bad guy was left behind. Michelangelo hit him with his *nunchucks.*

BLOOP!

A weird pink blob popped out of his chest. The bad guy was really a robot with a brain! The brain scurried away before Michelangelo could show anyone. His brothers didn't believe him.

Back in the sewer, the Turtles told Splinter about the failed rescue attempt.

"I need to train you as a team," Splinter said. "Next year you can go to the surface again."

But Donatello couldn't wait. He wanted to save April right away.

Splinter nodded. "Then you will need a leader." He chose Leonardo.

The next night, the Turtles returned to the streets. They found the van. Raphael wanted to attack immediately, but Leonardo said they should be patient. They waited and watched. The van drove off, and the Turtles followed it . . . to the bad guys' hideout.

The Turtles snuck into the hideout. They discovered that Michelangelo was right—the bad guys really were brain-like aliens! The aliens were called the Kraang, and they wanted April's dad, who was a famous scientist, to help them with an evil plan.

Some Kraang forced April and her dad into a helicopter. As it took off, Donatello leaped onto one of its landing skids to stop them. The copter spun and rocked. April fell out.

Donatello saved April, but the Kraang flew away with her dad.

"Looks like we'll have to fight our way out," said Leonardo. "It's about time," growled Raphael. The Turtles sprang into battle. They fought as a team, and they were unstoppable.

Suddenly, Leonardo had an idea. He ran to the hideout's power generator. The Kraang turned their blasters toward him and fired.

Leonardo jumped aside at the last second.

KABLAAM!

The generator exploded and destroyed the hideout as the Turtles and April tumbled away from the blast.

The Turtles returned to the safety of their secret lair. April was safe, but the Kraang still had her father.

"We won't rest until we find him," Donatello told her.

"We?" asked April. "This isn't your fight."

"It is now," said Donatello. "Because we are a team!"